WITHDRAWN FROM
COLLECTION

GHOST DETECTORS

As It Lies!

BOOK 22

BY
JAN FIELDS

ILLUSTRATED BY
DAVE SHEPHARD

Calico

An Imprint of Magic Wagon
abdopublishing.com

For all the fantastic people who edit my work and make me look so good. — JF

To Japhy, for holding so many silly poses while I draw. — DS

abdopublishing.com

Published by Magic Wagon, a division of ABDO, PO Box 398166, Minneapolis, Minnesota 55439. Copyright © 2018 by Abdo Consulting Group, Inc. International copyrights reserved in all countries. No part of this book may be reproduced in any form without written permission from the publisher. Calico™ is a trademark and logo of Magic Wagon.

Printed in the United States of America, North Mankato, Minnesota.
092017
012018

Written by Jan Fields
Illustrated by Dave Shephard
Edited by Bridget O'Brien
Designed by Christina Doffing

Publisher's Cataloging-in-Publication Data

Names: Fields, Jan, author. | Shephard, Dave, illustrator.
Title: As it lies! / by Jan Fields; illustrated by Dave Shephard.
Description: Minneapolis, Minnesota : Magic Wagon, 2018. | Series: Ghost detectors; Book 22
Summary: After a father-son miniature golf tournament is cancelled due to ghost-related incidents, the boys sneak into the park with Grandma Eunice to zap the ghost.
Identifiers: LCCN 2017946456 | ISBN 9781532131547 (lib.bdg.) | ISBN 9781532131646 (ebook) | ISBN 9781532131691 (Read-to-me ebook)
Subjects: LCSH: Ghost stories--Juvenile fiction. | Miniature golf--Juvenile fiction. | Grandparents--Juvenile fiction. | Humorous Stories--Juvenile fiction.
Classification: DDC [FIC]--dc23
LC record available at https://lccn.loc.gov/2017946456

Contents

Chapter 1
Ghoulie Golf

Malcolm stared across the dinner table, his mouth open. For once, he wasn't trying to gross out his sister, Cocoa. He was shocked. He snapped his mouth shut, swallowed, and said, "What?"

His father barely looked up from his plate of noodle surprise. "You and I are taking part in the father-son miniature golf tournament at the park this weekend. Dandy's father called and told me about it. I signed us up. You'll have fun."

"I'm fairly sure you promised me that when you made me go camping," Malcolm said. "I was squashed in the car with Dandy, squashed in a pup tent with Dandy, and fed burnt hot dogs."

"No one told you to drop your hot dog in the fire. Besides, you had fun. You might as well admit it."

Actually he *did* have fun, but not because they were dragged out into the wilderness. He had fun because they found a ghost. He almost smiled remembering it, but he didn't want Dad to think he was giving in.

"That doesn't mean I'll have fun playing golf," Malcolm said.

His dad frowned. "I don't know why you're acting so weird about this."

Beside him, Cocoa snorted. "He's a weirdo. That's all the reason he needs."

Mom gave Cocoa *the look*. "That's not helpful."

"Why are you picking on me?" Cocoa whined. "You always take his side."

"That's not helpful either," Mom said.

"Not helpful," Grandma Eunice echoed. Malcolm wasn't sure if she knew what was going on. His great-grandmother was busy staring at her plate. She was stabbing her food with her fork as if she thought something might be hiding underneath.

Grandma Eunice pretended to be loopy to get out of chores. Sometimes she even drooled. Of course, even when she wasn't pretending, Grandma Eunice wasn't exactly *normal*.

Malcolm took a deep breath, put his hands on the table, and tried to sound calm. "I had plans for this weekend."

He was planning to hang out in the basement working on his latest invention. Electronic glasses that let him see into the future. There would be no more flunked pop quizzes for him!

His father put down his fork. He and Malcolm faced one another across the table. The staring contest began. Malcolm knew this was a duel he had to win. Otherwise his weekend was going to be ruined.

His mom cut in. "Malcolm, you know this father-son tournament is important to Dandy. When you think about how much trouble you drag him into, I'm sure you'll choose to be supportive of his interests for once."

"Yeah," Cocoa said. "Think about someone besides yourself for once."

Malcolm considered throwing food at his sister, but he decided to ignore Cocoa instead. Leave it to Mom to hit him where it hurt.

Malcolm *did* drag Dandy into scary places. And they *did* end up in trouble a lot.

But that was the life of a Ghost Detector. Dandy understood that. Probably.

"This will be great," his father said. "The park has completely redesigned the miniature golf course. It's Ghoulie Golf now. That's your kind of place."

"Yeah," Cocoa said. "Creepy and gross." She shoved a spoonful of food into her mouth and chewed it with her mouth open.

"I am not the gross one," Malcolm yelled.

"Are too," Cocoa shouted back, spewing bits of noodle around.

"Aha!" Grandma Eunice crowed. She stabbed her plate so hard that it flipped over. Noodle surprise flew across the table and all over Cocoa.

Malcolm's sister launched out of her chair, screaming. Noodles hung in her hair, and sauce dripped from her nose.

In the middle of all the shouting and running around, Grandma Eunice calmly turned to Malcolm and gave him a wink. "It's only as bad as you make it."

Malcolm flopped back in his chair. He gave up. He'd spend his Saturday hitting little balls with a stick. But he wasn't going to like it!

Chapter 2
Attack of the Clown

"This will be the best day ever!" Dandy shouted for the third time in the short drive to the park. He also bounced in the seat so much that Malcolm was starting to feel a little carsick.

Dandy's dad laughed and put his hands over his ears. "I know you're excited. But this is a little car. You don't have to be so loud."

"Sorry," Dandy whispered, but he grinned at Malcolm. "Isn't this great?"

Malcolm forced the corners of his mouth up. "Super."

His dad gave him the stink eye in the rearview mirror. *What did he want?* Malcolm thought. Besides, Dandy didn't notice Malcolm's tone. He was too busy bouncing.

"I didn't know you liked golf."

Dandy stopped bouncing. "My cousin used to work at the Snack Shack next to the golf course. Sometimes we'd play after work." He shrugged. "That was before he went to college." He smiled so big Malcolm could almost count all his teeth.

Malcolm tried to think of something to distract Dandy before he started bouncing again. He pointed at Dandy's Ghoulie Golf T-shirt and hat. "Where did you get those?"

"An early bird prize," Dandy said. "I was the first kid who signed up."

Great, so I don't even get a shirt. Malcolm pressed his hands to his stomach as Dandy went back to bouncing.

Finally, they pulled into a parking space near the miniature golf course. Everyone piled out.

Malcolm leaned on the car, hoping fresh air would settle his stomach. He didn't want to hurl on the goofy clown head.

"Wow," Dandy said. "They changed everything."

For the first time, Malcolm really looked at the course. He had to admit, it looked cool. The peeling paint and broken fences he remembered from past visits were gone. The goofy clown now wore a creepy grin. The windmill hole had been turned into a haunted house with swirling specters flying around it. "It's okay."

Malcolm felt an arm slip around him. His dad yanked him into a sideways hug and bent down to whisper, "This is for Dandy. Be a good friend."

Malcolm swallowed hard. Dad could make whispering feel like yelling. He nodded and wriggled away. He'd show everyone what a good friend he could be. "Hey, Dandy. How's your backswing?"

Dandy blinked at him. "You don't really have a backswing in miniature golf. You just putt."

Malcolm thumped Dandy on the back. "Then let's get putting!"

It was hard keeping the happy face while they signed in and collected clubs and balls. A tall, skinny man stood at the edge of the golf course. His smile was wide and fake.

"Welcome to our first ever father-son golf tournament!" the man shouted. "I'm Karl Mashie, head of Parks and Recreation. We're going to have a great time today."

Malcolm's own fake smile slipped the rest of the way off. *Why does everyone keep saying that? What is so great about this?*

Mr. Mashie went over some boring rules. Malcolm passed the time by using his golf club to poke the other kids in line. When they turned around, he plastered an innocent look on his face. It was less boring than the speech, but it was still boring.

Finally, they got started. That's when Malcolm got his biggest surprise of the day. Dandy smacked the ball perfectly through a tunnel and into the hole in one shot.

"Wow." Malcolm slapped Dandy on the back. "That was awesome."

Dandy grinned and scratched his neck. "That was a lucky shot."

If it was a lucky shot, Dandy's luck stayed amazing. Malcolm had to hit the ball over and over every time. But Dandy never took more than three swats.

When they reached the hole with the big, creepy clown, Malcolm stopped and looked Dandy over carefully. "Did you find some kind of lucky charm?"

"He doesn't need luck," Dandy's dad said proudly. "He practices."

Really? Malcolm looked at Dandy in surprise. *Wow. A world where Dandy was really good at a sport.* Malcolm couldn't imagine it. Then he figured it out. "Of course," he said. "This is a dream."

Dandy looked at him with his mouth hung open. "You think so?"

"Of course it is," Malcolm said. "I'll prove it." He reached out and pinched Dandy.

"Ouch!" Dandy yelped. "How come I'm the one who gets pinched?"

"Right," Malcolm said. *I could have dreamed that Dandy yelped.* He took a deep breath and pinched himself hard on the arm. "Ow!"

Dandy grinned. "So I'm not dreaming. I'm winning."

"I guess." It was still weird. Just then, a golf ball whizzed by Malcolm's ear. "Hey, who hit that?"

Another ball zipped by Malcolm and smacked Dandy in the stomach. "Oof!"

Malcolm looked around. The big, creepy clown puckered up and spat out another ball. It flew right at Dandy's head. Malcolm pulled him out of the way. "It's the clown!"

The clown began spitting out balls faster and faster. One knocked Dandy's dad's hat off. Another hit a kid wearing one of the Ghoulie Golf T-shirts.

The dads hustled the boys away from the clown and the flying golf balls. When everyone was off the course, the clown seemed to run out of balls.

"Sorry folks," Mr. Mashie yelled as he hurried over. "Some kind of malfunction. We'll get it fixed right away. While you wait, everyone can have a free small drink at the Snack Shack."

The kids cheered and rushed to the Snack Shack. Malcolm looked back at the clown. It wasn't spitting golf balls. But as Malcolm stared at it, the clown gave him a slow, creepy wink.

Chapter 3
Up, Up, and Away

Malcolm stared at the clown face. "A ghost. It has to be a ghost."

"Malcolm, come on," his dad yelled. "We have to get in line."

Malcolm ran past Dad and soon caught up with Dandy. He leaned in close to his friend. "I think the clown is haunted."

Dandy stopped and poked Malcolm in the chest. "No. No ghosts. No haunting. This is my chance to win something. Stop trying to turn it into a Ghost Detector job."

Malcolm held up his hands. "It's not me. I didn't throw golf balls."

The dads caught up with them then. "No one thinks you threw any golf balls," Malcolm's dad said.

"I'm sure they'll fix the clown right away," Dandy's dad said.

Malcolm wasn't so sure. But Dandy had his arms crossed over his chest. Malcolm knew his friend was going to be stubborn about this. "Fine," Malcolm said. "Let's get a drink."

By the time they reached the front of the line, Malcolm was super thirsty. He hung on the counter and gasped out his order. The teenager on the other side of the counter laughed. "Sure thing, kid. Don't die on us."

The teenager shoved a cup under the soda machine and pushed the button. A blast of

orange soda shot out. It missed Malcolm completely and sprayed Dandy full in the face.

Malcolm pulled Dandy down below the counter. He crawled out of range of the drink machine. Dandy crawled behind him. Finally they both stood up.

"Now do you believe me?" Malcolm asked. "This place is haunted."

He looked around and pointed at the bike rack. "We can borrow some bikes and go home to get the specter detector and the ghost zapper. We can get rid of the ghost while everyone is drinking their soda."

Dandy wiped his dripping face on his wet shirt. "No."

"No what?"

"No everything." Dandy twisted the bottom of his soggy Ghoulie Golf shirt. Soda dripped on the ground. "I'm going to play golf."

"But the ghost!"

Dandy stamped his foot. "It's my turn to pick what we do. We always chase ghosts. Now we're going to play golf. And we're going to enjoy it." Dandy marched back to the golf course.

Malcolm ran after him. He had to talk some sense into Dandy.

Dandy headed for the big clown head. Two men poked at the head and muttered to each other. "Is it fixed yet?" Dandy asked.

One of the men twitched his moustache. "I guess. We can't find anything wrong with it."

"Maybe you better skip this hole, kid," the other man said as he gave the clown another poke. "Until we can figure it out."

Dandy scratched at his neck again. "I don't know, Malcolm. I don't think I can skip a hole."

Malcolm hauled Dandy away from the clown. "Let's give these guys room to work." As soon as they were far enough away, he whispered, "Did you hear them? They can't find what's wrong, because it's a ghost."

"Stop it!" Dandy yelled at him. Head down, he stomped over to the giant haunted house with the ghostly paddles.

The windmill paddles turned slowly as Dandy stalked toward them. The paddles began to twitch. They curled forward like the petals of a flower. Malcolm yelled, "Dandy, look out!"

Dandy didn't even look up. He just flapped a hand at Malcolm. When he got close enough to the windmill, the paddles reached toward Dandy. They couldn't reach. The paddle closest to the bottom began to stretch.

"Dandy!" Malcolm screamed.

His friend finally turned. "What?"

The stretched paddle hooked under the back of Dandy's soggy T-shirt. As the windmill kept turning, the paddle lifted Dandy off his feet.

"Help!"

Malcolm ran over. He yelled up to his friend, "I told you this place was haunted."

Before Dandy could answer, the dads arrived. Dandy had just passed the highest part of the windmill and was beginning to spin closer. Dandy's dad reached up and grabbed one of Dandy's legs. Malcolm's dad grabbed the other. As the blade spun lower, they unhooked Dandy's shirt.

"How did you manage to get caught on the windmill, Dandy?" his dad asked.

Dandy scowled. "It was an accident."

"We're having too many accidents today," Dandy's dad said.

At that, Mr. Mashie ran over. "You boys shouldn't play on the windmill."

"I wasn't on it," Dandy said. Then he scratched his neck. "Well, I was, but it wasn't my idea."

Mr. Mashie looked at Malcolm. "It's a dangerous place to play."

"It wasn't my idea either," Malcolm said.

Mr. Mashie sighed. "Fine. It looks like we have some fine-tuning to do on the course. And the Snack Shack. I'm going to send everyone home."

"Are you canceling the tournament?" Malcolm asked, trying not to sound too happy about it.

"No, we just need to work on some things." Mr. Mashie smiled at them. "I'm

sure it'll be fine tomorrow. I'll let everyone know."

Dandy grabbed Malcolm's arm and dragged him away from their dads. "I don't want the tournament canceled. We have to get rid of the ghost."

Malcolm grinned at his best friend. "Just what I wanted to hear. The Ghost Detectors are on the case!"

Chapter 4
Glow in the Dark

"We'll get rid of the ghost," Malcolm promised. "We always do."

"Yeah, Malcolm," Dandy grumbled. "We always do."

Malcolm didn't know why Dandy was so grumpy. The dads spent the rest of the day trying to cheer him up. Dandy moped through fishing at Miller's Pond. To be honest, so did Malcolm.

Could there be anything more boring than fishing? The only exciting part was

when bees started chasing Dandy. Dad said they wanted the dried soda in Dandy's shirt.

Dandy also moped through lunch, a trip to the movies, and dinner at Malcolm's house. Mom even washed his Ghoulie Golf shirt, but it didn't help much. This was the longest mope Dandy ever had.

The boys went to Malcolm's basement lab after dinner. Malcolm turned on the Ecto-Handheld-Automatic-Heat-Sensitive-Laser-Enchanced Specter Detector.

Yip! Yip! Malcolm's ghost dog Spooky popped into the room and danced around. Malcolm was glad someone was happy.

Dandy sure wasn't. "All I wanted was this one thing without a ghost wrecking it." He flopped down into Malcolm's beanbag chair. Spooky tried to jump into

Dandy's lap. He fell through Dandy's legs and disappeared into the beanbag chair.

Yip! Yip! The little dog popped out the side of the bag.

Dandy reached down to almost pat Spooky's head. "I didn't mean you, Spooky."

Malcolm really didn't want to spend Sunday playing golf. But he hated seeing Dandy miserable. "We can get rid of the ghost tonight. Then you'll be able to win your trophy tomorrow."

"How are we supposed to do that?" Dandy asked. "The park closes at sunset."

"Don't worry." Malcolm folded his arms over his chest. "That ghost is toast."

"Toast?" Dandy scratched the back of his neck. "You saw ghost toast? I only saw soda."

"No, I mean the ghost is going down."

"Going down where?"

Malcolm looked long and hard at his friend. "Don't you watch any cop shows?"

Dandy shrugged. "Not so much, but I like toast. What show is that on?"

Malcolm groaned and hauled his friend to his feet. "Forget it. You need to call home and say you're spending the night. Then after everyone is asleep, we're going ghost hunting."

"I want the ghost gone," Dandy complained, "but why do we have to go at the scariest possible time?"

"Because no one knows we're Ghost Detectors," Malcolm said as they headed up the basement stairs. "It's like our secret identity."

"I'd rather be Batman," Dandy grumbled.

They almost made it to the phone, but Malcolm's mom spotted them and pointed at Malcolm. "Take out the garbage."

"It's Cocoa's turn," Malcolm insisted.

"No, it's not!" his sister shrieked from the next room.

"No," his mother said as she spun Malcolm around and pointed him toward the garbage can. "It's not."

"Fine." Malcolm held his nose and stomped on the lever to open the can. Noodle surprise definitely didn't smell better after sitting in the garbage all day.

"Pee-yoo," Dandy said, pinching his nose.

They hauled the bag out of the can and tied it at the top. A little bit of noodle surprise spilled on the floor while they figured out how to tie the bag with one

hand. Cleaning the floor wasn't on his chore list. So, Malcolm pretended he didn't see the smelly glop.

Outside, one of the back door lights buzzed and popped and then went out entirely. "Great," Malcolm grumbled.

Malcolm hefted the bag higher and walked across the lawn, hoping he hadn't left anything out there to step on.

"Can I stay here?" Dandy suggested.

"In horror movies, monsters eat people right outside the door," Malcolm said.

Dandy stomped up behind him and grabbed the back of Malcolm's shirt. "Fine, but I'm not getting lost in the dark."

"We're only going to the garbage cans," Malcolm said.

When they were almost to the cans, both boys jumped as one of the cans suddenly

crashed to the ground. Something brushed by them, chittering as it ran. Dandy screamed and climbed up Malcolm's back.

"Hey, get off," Malcolm huffed.

"No way," Dandy yelled in Malcolm's ear. "There's something down there."

"It's a raccoon," Malcolm said. "They get in the garbage." He staggered a couple feet, struggling to keep his balance. "If you don't get off, I'm going to fall."

"Don't fall!" Dandy ordered. Malcolm fell anyway. They landed right in the stinky spilled garbage.

"Whoooo-ee," Malcolm said. "That's worse than old noodle surprise."

Malcolm set the garbage can upright again and put in the new bag. He slammed the lid on and put a rock on top of it. "Got it. Now we go call your parents."

On the way back to the house, Malcolm followed Dandy. He saw something glowing on the back of Dandy's neck. "Hold on!"

"Why?" Dandy asked. "I want to get inside."

"I think you have garbage stuck to your neck." Malcolm poked the glowing spot.

"Scrape it off," Dandy said. "That spot has been itching all day. I don't want it to get worse."

Malcolm squinted at the glowing spot. There were glowing letters on the back of Dandy's neck. He felt a chill raise goose bumps on his arms as he read the word out loud. "Never."

Chapter 5
Three is a Crowd

"Never what?" Dandy asked as he scratched at the letters.

"I don't know. That's all it says." Malcolm hauled his friend toward the house. "I want to look at it in the light."

Once they got in the kitchen, the letters didn't glow anymore. Instead, Dandy had a rash on his neck in that spot. "When did it start itching?" Malcolm asked.

"At the park," Dandy said. "I thought something bit me."

Dandy was always scratching or sniffling or sticking his fingers in his ears. Malcolm didn't even notice most of the time. But this looked ghost related to him. "When we zap this ghost, I think it'll stop itching."

A cranky voice barked behind them. "What's itching? Do you have fleas now?"

Malcolm turned, planning a comeback for his sister's snarky remark. Instead, both boys jumped. A furry, pink creature with a dripping green face smirked at them.

Malcolm grabbed Mom's cutting board and held it up like a shield. "Get back! Dandy, get the zapper."

"You two think you're so funny." The furry, pink creature put a hand on its hip. It certainly sounded like Cocoa. A blob of green dripped from its nose and onto the kitchen floor.

Mom walked in behind the creature. "Cocoa, you need to stay in the bathroom until you wash off the beauty mask. You're making a mess on the floor."

"That's a beauty mask?" Malcolm asked. "I'd hate to see an ugly mask."

"At least I don't have fleas," Cocoa snapped back.

Mom wrinkled her nose. "Are you sure that mask is fresh? Something smells."

"That's not me!" Cocoa shrieked.

Mom leaned over and sniffed Malcolm. Then she backed up. "Why do you both smell?"

"Because they're stinky boys," Cocoa sneered.

"Back to the bathroom, Cocoa," Mom snapped, pointing. "Go."

Cocoa flounced out of the kitchen.

"Don't forget to put Grandma Eunice's laundry in the bathroom when you're done," Mom yelled. Then she looked suspiciously at the boys. "Why do you smell?"

"It's been a long day. Can Dandy spend the night?" Malcolm asked.

"Of course." She pointed at Dandy. "Don't forget to call your parents." Then she wrinkled her nose again. "And be sure you both take baths."

After Cocoa was finally done in the bathroom, Malcolm and Dandy scrubbed the stink off. Then they settled down to wait until everyone in the house finally went to bed.

Malcolm crept over and opened the door. A growl came from down the hall.

"What's that?" Dandy squeaked.

"Just Dad snoring."

Malcolm grabbed the bag of Ghost Detector gear and tiptoed out. They almost made it.

"Hi boys!"

In the garage, Grandma Eunice sat in her wheelchair. She wore all black clothes and a battered football helmet on her head. She had tied herself into the chair with an old elastic bandage and was looping one end of a rope around the seat of Malcolm's bike.

Malcolm couldn't believe his eyes. "What are you doing?"

"When I heard about the crazy stuff at the park, I knew there was a ghost. And you're planning to zap it. I'm going too."

"I know you like to help," Malcolm said. "But you can't ride a bike, and we can't push you that far."

"You won't have to. I have a better idea."

Grandma Eunice held up the free end of the rope. Malcolm didn't know what Grandma Eunice had in mind, but he had a bad feeling about it.

He was right.

Chapter 6
Slingshot Grandma

"**Y**ou can't come," Malcolm said.

Grandma Eunice folded her arms. "You boys need me. I was a big help in the haunted doll case."

"She did help," Dandy agreed. "I think she should come."

"Don't think so much," Malcolm growled.

"If you don't let me come, I'll call your mother." Grandma Eunice pulled out her cell phone.

"Fine," he whispered fiercely. "But we are not pushing you."

"You're not," Grandma Eunice agreed. "You're pulling." She handed over the rope. "Tie this to Dandy's bike. I'll hold the middle of the rope, and you can tow me."

Getting started was hard. Malcolm had to stand on the bike pedals to get them turning. But once they were moving, he started to think they could do this.

He turned to look behind him. Even with the football helmet on, Malcolm could see Grandma Eunice grinning.

At least the last half of the trip is downhill, Malcolm thought as he began puffing. Beside him, Dandy gasped too.

Malcolm didn't know how they'd steer Grandma Eunice around traffic. Luckily they didn't see any cars. They passed a man

walking his dog. Grandma Eunice waved at him like she was part of a parade.

They were going downhill. Malcolm would have cheered except he didn't have enough air for the job. The bikes sailed along faster and faster. They didn't even need to pedal.

The wheelchair rolled faster too.

Malcolm looked back. Grandma Eunice was gaining on them. "Go faster, Dandy!"

They pedaled faster and faster. Everything was a blur of speed. Grandma Eunice whooped with excitement. She sounded close. Really close. He pedaled faster.

At the bottom of the hill, Malcolm could see the turnoff to the park. "We can't make that turn," he yelled to Dandy. "We have to slow down."

The bikes slowed down. The wheelchair didn't.

Grandma Eunice zipped in between them. "This is awesome!"

Right up until we all die, Malcolm thought. "Don't you have any brakes?" he shouted to her.

"At the back of the wheelchair," Grandma Eunice said. Then she passed them and the ropes grew tight. Now Grandma Eunice

was pulling the bikes instead of the bikes pulling her.

When they got to the park entrance, Grandma Eunice leaned hard to one side. The wheelchair reared up on one wheel. That made it turn.

She flew into the park. The bikes followed. On the park paths, Grandma Eunice stuck out her feet to slow down.

The boys mashed their brakes, but they'd worn them out on the hill. They were heading straight for the park fountain. And they couldn't stop.

Chapter 7
Squish Cheez & Flowers

Malcolm and Dandy passed Grandma Eunice. Their bikes hit the edge of the fountain and stopped. Malcolm and Dandy didn't.

They sailed over the handlebars and into the fountain. Sputtering and spitting, Malcolm sat up in the freezing water. "Dandy?"

Dandy coughed. "Right here!"

Both boys looked back at Grandma Eunice, sitting dry and safe in her

wheelchair. She flung out her arms and yelled, "Ta-da!"

Malcolm and Dandy waded out of the water. They untied their battered bikes from Grandma Eunice. She poked Malcolm. "Don't mope. No harm done."

He just looked at her for a moment. "You know we're stuck here, right? We can't possibly pull you up that hill."

"You worry too much." She pulled the helmet off her head and a flashlight out of her pocket. She flashed it in Malcolm's eyes. "Where's the ghost?"

The boys began pushing Grandma Eunice along the park paths. As they got closer to the golf course, they stopped. "You better stay here," Malcolm said.

"We do a lot of running when ghosts show up," Dandy added.

"Forget it. You boys need me." Grandma Eunice began rolling herself toward the golf course.

Malcolm hurried to pass her. He was still in charge of the Ghost Detectors!

He pulled the specter detector out of his backpack and turned it on. Nothing appeared. The only sounds were the soft creak of the windmill as it turned and the squish of their wet sneakers as they walked.

"Looks like the ghost is playing hide-and-seek," Grandma Eunice said. "I love hide-and-seek."

"I like the hiding part," Dandy added as he peeked around the wheelchair.

"Well, if it wants to hide," Malcolm said, "we have to seek. And then we zap." He handed the specter detector to Grandma Eunice. Then he rooted around in his bag

for the Ecto-Handheld-Automatic-Heat-Sensitive-Laser-Enchanced Ghost Zapper. He couldn't find it.

Then he felt the metal can that had to be the ghost zapper. He pulled out a can of Squish Cheez.

"Oh, yum," Dandy said. "Squish Cheez!"

Malcolm tossed Dandy the can. He poked and pushed and rooted in his backpack. Finally he dumped out the contents on the path. "Where's the ghost zapper?"

Grandma Eunice raised her hand. "I borrowed your ghost zapper when I heard something howling outside my window last week. It was just a cat."

"And you didn't put it back?"

"I put that in the bag to remind me to put the zapper back." Grandma Eunice shrugged. "I guess it didn't work."

Malcolm groaned. What were they going to do? Even if they found the ghost, they couldn't zap it. And they couldn't go home either. With a sigh, he said, "Let's keep looking."

The group continued down the paths between the different holes. They stayed well away from the windmill, but Dandy still twitched every time it creaked.

"I don't know why they made all these changes," Grandma Eunice said. "This was a perfectly nice golf course before."

As soon as she said that, the ghost detector beeped. A ghostly glowing flower appeared in the air above her wheelchair.

"What's that?" Dandy yelped.

The flower floated into Grandma Eunice's lap. When she touched it, it vanished. The ghost detector stopped beeping.

"This ghost doesn't seem too bad," she said.

"Wait until you're hoisted into the air," Dandy grumbled.

"Don't give the ghost any ideas," Malcolm warned.

"Look," Grandma Eunice said, pointing at another ghostly flower hanging in the air. She went after it, rolling her wheelchair right across the painted greens of the course.

"Wait!" Malcolm yelled. "It might be a trap!"

Chapter 8
Going Batty!

When Grandma Eunice didn't stop, Malcolm and Dandy ran after her. Grandma Eunice could really roll!

"You said this is a trap," Dandy whispered. "Why are we following her?"

"Because we're Ghost Detectors," Malcolm said. "We don't let a member of the team go it alone."

"You can leave me behind. I'll wait."

Malcolm grabbed Dandy and hauled him along. He had to keep them all together.

Suddenly Dandy's arm jerked out of Malcolm's grip. "Help!"

Malcolm whirled around. A wooden skull held Dandy's foot clamped between glowing white teeth. Dandy thumped on the top of the skull with the can of Squish Cheez. "Let go!"

Malcolm grabbed the can from Dandy. He shoved it between the skull's jaws and pried them open. Dandy pulled out his foot. "You used to be my favorite hole."

The skull just squeezed the can of cheese and grinned.

Then they looked around. "Where's Grandma Eunice?"

The glowing flower was gone. So was Grandma Eunice. The ghost had her!

"Grandma Eunice!" Malcolm yelled. All he heard was the squeak of the windmill.

The boys searched the course, but they couldn't find Grandma Eunice.

Then Dandy pointed a shaky finger at the one place they hadn't looked. It was a fake cave where players putted the last hole in the dark. The cave was lit by black lights which made the white golf balls glow.

Malcolm looked to the cave entrance. He saw Grandma Eunice's football helmet on the fake green grass.

Dandy scratched the back of his neck again. "Maybe she's just looking around inside. We could wait for her to come out. I don't mind waiting."

"No." Malcolm pushed Dandy's hand away so he could see the rash on his neck. The letters glowed brightly. Then as Malcolm looked, the letters seemed to move and change. "Stop scratching for a second."

Dandy scratched anyway. "Dude, it itches like crazy!"

Again Malcolm pulled his friend's hand away. He could read the newly formed letters. Malcolm read the message aloud. "Stay Out!"

"Sounds like good advice to me," Dandy said.

"Fine," Malcolm snapped. "Stay out here all alone in the dark."

He stomped toward the cave. In seconds, he heard Dandy's footsteps right behind him. Inside the cave, strings of fake cobwebs hung from the ceiling. They tickled Malcolm's neck, and he shuddered.

The black lights were on, which gave the cobwebs a creepy glow. *Why would the ghost turn on the lights?*

"Grandma Eunice!" Malcolm yelled.

The words echoed around him. But from deeper in the cave, he heard, "Malcolm?"

"We're coming!" Malcolm yelled. The cave floor was full of bumps and bulges meant to make it harder for the golfers to reach the center of the cave. Now they just tripped the boys as they tried to hurry.

Then he heard loud squeaking.

"Is that the wheelchair?" Dandy asked.

It wasn't. A mass of glowing lights moved around near the ceiling up ahead.

Squee! Squee!

"Ghost bats!" Malcolm yelled.

The bats swooped down at them. The boys screamed and ran with their arms shielding their heads. If he had his ghost zapper, Malcolm could blast the bats. But without it, screaming and running was the best he could come up with.

Malcolm and Dandy stumbled out of
the cave, but the bats didn't follow them.
"I guess they just wanted us to leave,"
Malcolm said.

Dandy nodded so much he looked like a bobblehead doll. "That's what I want too."

Malcolm pointed to the cave. "Grandma Eunice is in there."

"Yes," Dandy agreed. "But the ghost gave her flowers. It gave us bats and rashes and biting teeth."

"We need some kind of protection," Malcolm said. "I wonder if the golf course has a toolshed."

"There's a storage room in the back of the Snack Shack," Dandy said.

"How did you know that?"

Dandy shrugged. "My cousin worked there, remember?"

"Then let's go see what we can find." Malcolm yelled back into the dark bat cave. "We'll be back soon, Grandma Eunice!"

No sound came from the cave at all.

Chapter 9
Knights to the Rescue

The Snack Shack was locked up for the night, but Dandy produced a key from a crack in the side of the door frame. Once inside, they slipped into the storeroom.

Malcolm shone his flashlight beam around. Mostly they found extra bags of chips and jugs of soda syrup. None of it looked like it would be very good for fighting off bats.

Then they squeezed by a tall stack of boxes and found two towering suits of

armor in the corner. "Knights?" Malcolm asked. "I didn't remember any knights in the park."

"They were next to the castle hole," Dandy said. "I think there's a Frankenstein monster there now."

"This is better than monsters." Malcolm shoved a helmet on his friend's head. It took a lot of pushing. Dandy had a big head.

"Ouch!" Dandy yelped. "Not so hard."

"Do you want to go back in that cave without a helmet?"

Dandy pushed the visor open on the helmet. "I don't want to go back in that cave at all."

"We have to save Grandma Eunice!" Malcolm put on his own helmet.

The boys soon learned the rest of the armor was too rusty and bent to wear. "We

can just wear the helmets," Malcolm said. "That should be enough to keep the bats off our heads."

The helmets made it hard to see. The boys stumbled out of the Snack Shack without running into anything except each other. Once outside, Malcolm grabbed the lids from the trash cans behind the building.

"Shields!" he said, handing one to Dandy.

Dandy waved his hand in front of his helmet. "Stinky shields."

They walked as fast as they could, but the helmets were heavy. Both boys were panting by the time they got to the cave. "This helmet is making me sweat," Dandy complained.

"You'll thank me when those bats come back." Malcolm turned on his flashlight

and headed into the cave. "Now let's go find Grandma Eunice."

Dandy opened his mouth to yell for Grandma Eunice, but Malcolm quickly shushed him. "Quiet. We don't need the ghost to know we're in here." He started along the twisting cave tunnels.

"I still don't know what we're going to do about the ghost," Dandy whispered. "We don't have the ghost zapper."

"We'll think of something."

Malcolm wished he had some ideas. They didn't always zap the ghosts they found. Sometimes the ghosts left on their own. But Malcolm didn't think this ghost was going to do that. "We need to figure out why the ghost is haunting this place."

Dandy scratched his neck. Malcolm could still see a glow peeking out from

under the helmet. "Maybe he just liked golf."

"Then why scare people away who want to play?" Malcolm asked.

"Maybe the ghost hated golf?" Dandy suggested.

"Maybe."

Malcolm thought it might be more than that. He thought about the way the golf balls only shot out after Dandy got near the clown. And how the soda machine only sprayed Dandy. And how the windmill grabbed Dandy.

"The ghost was after you," Malcolm said. "You're the one it targeted every single time. Well, except with the flowers. But I don't think that was the same thing at all."

"Me?" Dandy yelped. "Why would it be after me?"

Malcolm stopped and looked at his friend. "Maybe the ghost doesn't like skinny kids with big heads?"

"Hey! My head isn't that big."

"It took three pushes to get that helmet on you."

"Maybe knights had teeny tiny heads," Dandy grumbled.

Malcolm remembered Dandy's dad had a big head too, but the ghost had ignored him. Then Malcolm pointed at Dandy's damp, dirty shirt.

"What about my shirt?" Dandy looked down. His helmet banged into Malcolm's head with a clang.

After the ringing stopped in their heads, Malcolm risked pointing at the shirt again. "I think that's the reason we're being haunted."

Dandy looked up at him. "Huh? You think the ghost hates T-shirts?"

"I think the ghost hates Ghoulie Golf," Malcolm said. "You're one of the few people wearing the Ghoulie Golf T-shirt, so it picked on you."

"Why would it hate Ghoulie Golf?" Dandy asked. "Everyone loves Ghoulie Golf."

Malcolm peered into the darkness ahead and shivered. Someone definitely didn't love Ghoulie Golf. And that someone had Grandma Eunice.

Chapter 10
Par for the Course

Malcolm stopped so suddenly that Dandy ran into him. "Shush!" Malcolm hissed and turned off the flashlight. Darkness slammed down on them.

"Why'd you do that?" Dandy demanded.

"Look." Malcolm pointed ahead, then realized Dandy probably couldn't see his finger. But surely he could see the glow coming from ahead in the tunnel.

"Is that the way out?" Dandy asked.

He took a step ahead and Malcolm could see the glowing letters on the back of Dandy's neck. "Nope!" they said.

Malcolm swallowed hard. "The ghost knows we're here."

"Then let's hurry up and get out." Dandy trotted ahead before Malcolm could grab him. With no better idea, Malcolm followed.

The glow wasn't the end of the tunnel. It came from a gazillion ghostly candles floating around a little table. Grandma Eunice sat in her wheelchair next to the table. She spotted the boys and waved. "About time you two got here."

From the other side of the table, a ghost glared at the two boys.

"Are you all right, Grandma Eunice?" Malcolm asked.

"Of course," she said. "I've been telling Freddie that he needs to stop haunting the golf course."

"*My* golf course," the ghost grumbled.

"Why are you haunting your own golf course?" Malcolm asked.

"Because they ruined it!" The ghost tried to slam his hand down on the ghostly table, but it passed right through. "I designed the best course in the state! I had the tallest windmill, the happiest clown, and this." He waved his hands around. "Who else has a gold mine? And now it's ruined!"

The ghost tried to pound the table again. The floating candles turned into ghost bats and flew around their heads.

Grandma Eunice leaned over the table and smacked the ghost on the nose with her flashlight. The flashlight passed right

through him, but he still looked surprised. "Stop it," Grandma Eunice scolded. "I don't want bats in my hair."

The bats changed back to candles as the ghost slumped in his chair. "They made my beautiful golf course look scary, so I made it scary. No one will want to play here."

"Scary can be fun," Malcolm said.

"I was looking forward to playing here for weeks," Dandy said.

"You were?" the ghost said. Then he frowned again and pointed at Dandy's shirt. "Because it's Ghoulie Golf."

"No," Dandy said. "Because it's the best course ever. It's fun, but it's not too easy."

Malcolm noticed the ghost wasn't glaring anymore. "Putting the last hole in a cave is a brilliant idea," he added.

"It's a mine!" the ghost snapped.

Grandma Eunice swatted at him with her flashlight again. "The important thing is that these two are very excited to play on your course. So were the other kids and their dads. Isn't that why you built this course in the first place?"

The ghost crossed his arms over his chest and sulked for a few seconds. Finally he sighed. "Yeah. That's why I built it."

"Can't you let us have the tournament?" Dandy asked. "I was really looking forward to it."

Malcolm didn't want to waste another day on miniature golf, but he looked at Dandy's face. His friend really wanted to play. So he took a step toward the ghost and chimed in. "Please?"

The ghost looked from Malcolm to Dandy. "I guess I could."

Dandy tried to scratch his neck, but his fingers smacked the edge of his helmet. "Could you make this rash go away? It's so itchy."

The ghost winced. "Sure. I guess that was a little mean."

Malcolm saw the glow vanish from the back of Dandy's neck. His friend sighed with relief. "Thanks," he said.

"You know, I heard about you two," the ghost said. "How come you didn't just blast me with that zapping thing you have?"

Dandy opened his mouth to answer, but Grandma Eunice interrupted. "Blast someone who gave me flowers? Never."

And at that, the ghost finally smiled. "You could come see me sometime."

"Maybe," she said. "If you stop scaring children."

"Okay," the ghost said. Then he made a flower appear and he handed it to Grandma Eunice. The flower disappeared as soon as she touched it, but she still smiled.

When Malcolm and Dandy finally pushed her out of the haunted mine bat cave, Malcolm pointed toward the road. "There is no way we can push you home."

"No problem," Grandma Eunice said. "I've got it covered." She pulled out her cell phone and quickly made a call. "Oh? Did I wake you up?"

She held the phone away from her ear. Malcolm heard shouting through the phone. It sounded a lot like his mom.

When the shouting stopped, Grandma Eunice said, "I decided to go out for a hot dog." After more shouting, she added, "I'm at the Snack Shack. The boys are with me.

We need a ride." Then Grandma Eunice ended the call.

"Our ride should be here soon," she said.

"Mom is going to kill us," Malcolm said.

"Don't be silly. I'll tell her I made you boys come. I'm loopy, you know. You two will be heroes for looking after me." She pointed at the helmets. "You might want to put those back before anyone gets here."

Malcolm and Dandy took their helmets back to the Snack Shack. "You're going to be great in the tournament tomorrow," Malcolm said.

Dandy stared at him. "You really think so? I thought you didn't like golf."

"I don't," Malcolm said with a grin. "But I like you. That's all best friends need."

Dandy grinned back, and both boys walked out to wait for their ride home.

Questions for You

From Ghost Detectors
Malcolm and Dandy

Dandy: I can do bird calls and play miniature golf. Both those things surprised Malcolm. What are some surprising things you like to do?

Malcolm: Miniature golf was more fun than I expected. And Dandy even beat me! I'm glad Dad made me do it. What's something you had to do that you liked more than you thought you would?

Dandy: That ghost was really mad about the changes to his golf course. Has anyone ever thought you should change something you made? How did that make you feel?

Malcolm: Grandma Eunice sure has some wild ideas sometimes. What's the wildest idea you ever had?